Hassan's Zoo
&
A Village in Winter

Ruth Brandt

First published August 2021 by Fly on the Wall Press
Published in the UK by Fly on the Wall Press
56 High Lea Rd
New Mills
Derbyshire
SK22 3DP

www.flyonthewallpress.co.uk
Copyright Ruth Brandt © 2021
ISBN: 9781913211462

Dedicated to my father, Bob Brandt, my sons Jack and Patrick and to Bill.

Acknowledgments

Hassan's Zoo was previously published in *Litro* Issue 107, June 2011. A Village in Winter (under the name of A Village Street in Winter) was previously published by *The Blue Nib*, March 2019.

Hassan's Zoo

For the first six days Hassan couldn't leave the house he shared with his mother, father and two younger sisters, Haja and Farrah. As explosions juddered the floor and the incessant high-pitched shrieks of missiles passed overhead, he worried that they would all die, suffocated by brick dust, their limbs crushed by chunks of rubble. Towards the end of those days, in carefully selected moments when the noise of warfare dulled, he permitted his heart to lilt with hope that the fighting might be over, and at these times he turned his thoughts away from what the future held for his family and towards the animals he should have been caring for.

He never doubted that the other zoo staff would be holed up in their houses too. The occasional visit from a neighbour with news of a ministry bombed, or a block taken, or a rumour passed stealthily from person to person that electricity would be available at seven that evening, invariably also told of city streets empty of civilians. Even doctors and nurses were staying away from hospitals where life-threatening injuries – plenty of these were discussed and grieved over – were left unattended to. What madness was taking place?

"Tomorrow will be better," Hassan's father would pacify the visitors and his family who, like him, could only envisage a brighter future.

"Shock and awe." His father shook his head as he said these words, as if he himself were in awe of the military operation taking place for their benefit.

By the seventh day, food supplies, gathered diligently during the preceding weeks of negotiation and searches for weapons of mass destruction, were becoming low and, although buckets, empty cans and even his youngest sister's dolls' prams were brimming with water, the daily half-hour gushes from the taps had ceased. The stench of urine and composting faeces could not be avoided, however far within the four walls Hassan roamed from their unflushable toilet. His ears had become immune to the frequent cascades of shots from outside. And with stories of young girls' purity being taken by troops from both sides proliferating, he found maintaining the high level of fear he had lived with for several days had become impossible. Any pity he had originally harboured for his mother's twitches and sobs had turned into irritation. Even his father's optimism had faded, leaving the man who could only foresee freedom and democracy self-consciously quiet and humbled.

"I'm going out," Hassan announced, at which his mother let out a predictable wail. "We'll be needing food soon," he reassured. "And I'll see if there's water anywhere."

Both of these were true, and it certainly was his intention to find whatever food there might be to bring home, but he also had a compulsion to get to his animals. He could imagine only too well the effect that a week of being confined without food and water, incomprehensible noises blasting, might be having at the zoo.

"I won't be long." He kissed his mother on her hair parting, patted his sisters' heads and finally shook his father's hand.

"Be careful," his father said and squeezed Hassan's hand a touch tighter than necessary for a goodbye.

That Hassan had wanted to be a vet since a child had never been a secret. Animals had always fascinated him; the sheer variety of them; the way they adapted to their environments; the simplicity with which, when left alone by man, they lived on and alongside nature. What was a slightly guilty secret, however, was that at twenty-one he still harboured this childish ambition. But as time had gone on, and his father's promotions still failed to materialise, and no stroke of luck arrived along with the necessary fees for his training, he had resigned himself to the fact that becoming a vet was an ambition unlikely to come to fruition. He had therefore endeavoured to content himself with his job as a zoo hand: chopping fruit for the apes; mucking out the elephants and giraffes; weeding the flower beds which filled the acres of land surrounding the eight hundred or so animals and birds. And as he worked, his general interest in animals focussed in on specific animals, namely those in the zoo. Even though he would never name a favourite, in the same way a parent would never name a favourite child, in his heart Kesari, the beautiful Bengal tiger, had a special place.

He found the street abnormally quiet. He darted from shadow to shadow, down alleys and through bombed buildings, pausing to listen, glancing at rooftops and round corners, his heart racing out of all proportion with the speed of his legs, and as he made slow, convoluted progress towards the zoo, his mind ran along the row of cages - four gorillas, six rhesus monkeys, a variety of parrots and budgerigars, three Labradors and a Beagle - then on to the bear enclosure containing the female American brown. And, ignoring the shattered debris all around him, he prayed to Allah that they would be unharmed.

9

The zoo gates, locked as usual the day before the invasion began, lay flat on the ground, padlock intact, the gate posts similarly prone. The ticket office was a hole, almost a mirror image of the single storey building that had once stood. Hassan balanced along the rubble that had been the wall and hopped down into the zoo grounds, surveying the scene.

In front of him, the first row of cages, so recently envisaged full of lively animals, were a twisted mass of metal rods. Away somewhere to his right, the scream of an unidentifiable animal in fear gripped at his heart and the reek of decomposition forced bile into his mouth. Slowly, methodically, as though carrying out a normal morning sweep of the paths, Hassan walked past the cages, searching for any evidence that creatures had once lived there. Only the buzzing of flies alerted him to a mass in the monkey cage so covered in dust that it could have been a stone. Hassan hurried past. Just the one corpse, he thought. The others will be free, scampering through trees, feeding off flowers and titbits they find lying around. He had some hope for the monkeys. In the next cage a lemur cringed, its remaining eye asking Hassan for water, for food. He held open his hands. He had nothing but he would find something. He'd be back.

A scuffle diverted him, low voices muttering over by the penguin enclosure. Hassan's heart sang out. Other zoo keepers were there. His colleagues had turned up to tend to the animals too. He ran, flitting between hiding places, his recently acquired ability to move discreetly in self-preservation already ingrained in him. He passed the lion enclosure, noting the cubs lying on their sides panting while their mother pawed the ground as if searching for roots to feed them. On past Kesari's cage where he paused while the elegant giant cat raised her head from the earth floor to growl. On he ran.

Two men, one with a canvas bag, stood by the miraculously intact wall next to the pit that had once been filled with water. Hassan steadied himself. These weren't men he knew. He faded into the darkness behind a tree.

"... better than that dog," he overheard.

The honking snore of a distressed penguin erupted from the bag. Incensed, Hassan stepped out from his hiding place and, surprising himself with his forwardness, after all these men could be carrying a knife or a gun, said:

"What have you got there?"

"It's ours." The man clutched at his bag.

Thinking only of the poor, captured creature, Hassan advanced on the men.

"It belongs to the zoo. I am a keeper here." A slight variation from the truth in these circumstances was surely permitted. "And I'm instructing you to put the bag down, now."

"Too late," the second man said.

"It's still alive," Hassan insisted, for while there was life, there was hope.

The first man shook his head.

"What can we do?" he asked. "We're hungry. My wife and children are hungry."

Only now did Hassan fully understand and his anger increased.

"You can't eat it," he said, the words sticking in his throat.

"Why not?" the second man asked. "If those other bastards can get their chops round a giraffe, why can't we eat a bird?"

"The giraffe?"

A shot from somewhere close killed the discussion and, in the second that Hassan retreated to the tree for protection, the men scarpered with the penguin. He quaked, waiting for who knew what.

The American soldiers walked backwards, sideways past him, their eyes looking everywhere all at once, taking in each twitch of a leaf, each dart of a fly. Hassan held his breath. One of them yelled out, pointed the butt of his gun in the direction of the animal stealers and they too were off. Hassan let the air stream into his lungs as he relaxed and, with the boot steps dimming, he sneaked out, knowing that his duty was to preserve what life he could.

Lifting the dead monkey was almost impossible. Its body barely hung together any longer with the flies and decay. Added to that, the smell repulsed Hassan more than anything had ever repulsed him before. He carried the corpse by a foot, holding it away from his body so as not to taint his clothes, (there would be no washing them for some time to come). Finally, he reached his destination and lobbed the animal he had once fed on dates into the lions' den. And then he was off. He had work to do.

Capturing the lemur wasn't hard. The creature had no energy to swing away to safety, and as he carried it, its head wrapped in his shirt, he pretended that it wasn't real. What else was he to do?

Kesari had moved to the bars as though anticipating Hassan's return and he was grateful for this, for somehow the tiger's action justified what he was about to do.

"Good girl," Hassan said, half to the tiger, half to the lemur. "Good girl."

Kesari backed away, distrusting Hassan. Would he not be her saviour after all? Yet even as he saw this withdrawal from him, Hassan hesitated.

"Good girl," he repeated, trying not to think.

It would have been easier if the lemur hadn't found a last bit of strength inside her, a primitive surge from deep within which remained when all else had deserted her.

"Go." He pushed her head through the bars. "Go," he shouted, unfurling the fingers that clasped.

And she was gone, and Hassan bowed his head and prayed to Allah for forgiveness.

A canal flowed past the zoo. In normal times Hassan had paid it little heed, since it was simply a city canal. Now it was the only source of water he knew of. Acquiring the buckets had been straightforward. The hotel which overlooked the zoo's gardens had lost its rear door, easy to walk into, easy to find the housekeeping cupboard, easy to pick up six buckets. He lay on the bank and swooshed up the fetid water. One, two, three buckets filled. Four, five, …

"Hey."

He jumped, the last bucket falling away into the water. Panic and fear shot down his arms as he rose to face the American whose gun, slung across his chest, was only a twist away from Hassan's head. He raised his hands, just like in the films, not comprehending the words being hurled at him. The shouting stopped, the soldier was expecting something from him in return. What was Hassan to do? He growled, pointing at the buckets, then the zoo. The American watched, his face showing no understanding, no emotion. Hassan repeated what might be his final act. The American looked at the water, looked at Hassan and spoke in a voice so huge that it resounded in Hassan's head, before picking up three of the buckets. Hassan followed with the remaining two, the stinking water spilling down his trousers.

Hassan was grateful to Kesari for leaving no trace of the lemur. Now he could pretend it had never happened. He lowered a bucket into the cage and, as she lapped, the soldier took off his backpack and pulled out a box which he ripped open to take out a foil packet, the contents of which the tiger consumed with one lick. Next out of the box came a bar of chocolate which the soldier handed almost carelessly to Hassan before tearing open another foil packet to feed to the tiger.

"Thank you," Hassan said, although he knew the soldier wouldn't understand. "I'll take it to my family, my sisters," he explained as he put it in his trouser pocket. "Haja and Farrah," he named them to demonstrate their thanks too. "Thank you."

Another soldier joined them, and another. One had brought a crate of rations with him. Hassan moved between cages, alerting the soldiers to the animals which needed feeding, those which needed water, those which, may Allah forgive him, were better off being fed to another. When all were counted only forty-three remained alive. One soldier patted him on the shoulder, another smiled and slapped him on the back and in his head he allowed himself to imagine that amongst these men would be one who would see his ability with the animals and who would say:

"Here, Hassan, why don't you come to the United States of America and study to be a vet? Our country will pay of course, after all, look what we've done to yours."

When evening arrived, and the carrying of water from the canal had ceased for the time being, Hassan sat with the soldiers. He couldn't understand a word they said, but was content in the safety his new friends provided and grateful to the men who had ensured some of his animals would live, for today at least. He had explained to them they needed donkeys to feed the big cats. Four dollars a donkey, he held up four fingers and said the word, "Dollar," he could manage that much English. They had copied his bray to show they understood and he had stood side by side with foreign soldiers and laughed.

Hassan couldn't linger long though. While there was still light, he had to leave his zoo and attempt the dangerous journey home to bring his family the four bars of chocolate he had now been given, together with two of the foil bags of food he had guiltily pocketed while no one was looking. His parents would be pleased with him. His sisters would be pleased with him. Tomorrow he would return and, while he continued to tend to his animals, he would start work on improving his English.

Some of the soldiers were smoking, some drinking alcohol from bottles. They were eating, offering him bits of food which he ate readily, but not too greedily, and because he was paying attention to the group, he didn't notice the lone soldier enter Kesari's cage until, as if someone had instructed them to, they all turned as one. In the cage the American held out his arm, taunting Kesari with a piece of meat.

"No," Hassan called, trying to smile. He didn't like to upset his new friends by shouting. "She's dangerous. Get out."

Momentarily the soldier turned to look at him and in that split second Kesari attacked, the man's fingers disappearing between the tiger's teeth.

The shot that cracked past Hassan's head was the loudest he had heard in all the fighting. Kesari's legs lost their bones, wobbling her body to the ground. Her head smacked onto the compacted dirt and, even seeing the blood spurting from beside her eye, Hassan couldn't believe that in this world turned upside down, Kesari was dead.

The soldiers became a trained fighting machine once more. The handless man was passed moaning over the cage bars. First-aid packs were opened. Hassan backed away from them all, the comradeship of a few minutes ago forgotten. And he remembered his mother driven mad by fear, his father's hopes betrayed, his vulnerable sisters. He wiped a week's tears from his cheeks with his stinking hand and as the chocolate in his pockets became rancid, he whispered to himself:

"You bastards," for Kesari's pointless death, for the death these men had brought to his country, and for the death of his dream.

A Village in Winter

For a couple of days that winter it blew warm. Half our street, the south-facing half, glinted with ochres and terracottas in the strobing sunlight, while the north-facing side radiated arctic blue. Uphill, land warmed by the unexpected heat gave up its water and the river began to rise. None of us worried much about the river. After all, for a brief while we had our street back to play in. Even Matt the Frost came out, loitering on his blue side of the street, posing spikey figures in its shadows, his bobble hat erect, his gloves pulled to the ends of his fingers, arms jittering, throat grunting.

"You kids, why don't you dance too?" Mrs Gregory suggested, as though it was up to us to lure Matt the Frost from the dark side. "Go on." She went as far as placing her radio on her doorstep.

Frizz, Sarah and I had no intention of dancing.

"He's mental," Frizz said.

If Sarah or I had said that, Mrs Gregory would have cuffed us. Instead, she pulled her coat close.

"Go on, Bun," she said to me.

I shrugged. What was the point?

It was Mr Drake who warned about the river. Nothing much, just a comment as he passed us by on the melted side of the street.

"Don't go near the banks, kids," he called.

The minute his door was shut we crossed the shadow's stark line to investigate. From behind a dark bush came a shuffling and the flick of a knitted hat. I paused. Was that Matt hissing or river water scraping through reeds?

"Hey," Sarah shouted, and I found I had been left behind in the shadow zone, alone with the scent of Matt the Frost.

I ran.

"What?" I called, glancing behind.

"Look."

A rug, a genuine green and blue patterned rug was rushing down the river.

"My granny's," Frizz said, but we all knew that Frizz had no granny. He had no dad either, just him and Matt and their mum, who never came out, not even with the sun.

"Matt most probably pissed on it," Sarah said.

"Crapped," I crouched to mimic.

They both laughed. See, Frizz didn't mind the joke being on his brother.

"I'm not fishing it out," Frizz said. "Not whoever's it is."

So we threw sticks and grass at it as it came near and then, when it did nothing but wallow in front of us in the current, Sarah and I turned to fart it on downstream.

"Better get home," Frizz said.

Frizz always had to get home.

"Go on then," Sarah said.

Over the next few days the weather stayed fine. We didn't go back to the river, mostly because Frizz didn't come out. Something or other about Matt, he told us through his window. All sorts of things Frizz told us, none of which ever seemed quite right.

Mrs Gregory said to leave Frizz and his mum be for a while. Stop pestering. That poor woman with that lad. Sarah and I skateboarded a bit. Did nothing mainly.

About the fifth day the air warmed till there was talk of it reaching season-change temperature. The sun rose earlier too, set later, and Matt the Frost reappeared, except his gloves were off, his hat nowhere to be seen. The sharp shapes he'd earlier pulled became curves and bends. Still the shade dominated their side of the street, still he remained in the grey glow of winter while on our side green blades sprouted in Mrs Gregory's front lawn.

"You," Sarah called. I don't know what she wanted. I don't suppose she did either. "You, frosty boy."

Matt just stood there, then jumped into a star, then curved into an S, and a shape that could have been a C and could have been an O. He dropped a shoulder and then a hip, lolloping like a puppet. No longer Matt the Frost, but Matt the Drip, curving and bending and melting.

"Mental," Sarah shouted.

"Mental," I copied.

"You two stop that!" Mrs Gregory called.

Sarah turned her back on Mrs Gregory's front window and squeezed a sloppy fart through her teeth.

I swear that Sarah was making this noise to Mrs Gregory. I swear that she wasn't pointing any of it at Matt, but for a moment he froze into angles and sparkles again, before wailing, like a child who's had his nose pulled. And then he ran, all elbows and heels, like no part of his body belonged to any other part, like he had been built from donated limbs and organs.

Sarah pissed herself laughing. I did too. We went back to our skateboards and paid no attention to where Matt had gone, never even thought of him till about ten minutes later when Frizz's door slammed and Frizz was out.

"Tosser," Sarah shouted into the gloom.

"Tosser," I copied.

"Got your skateboard?"

But Frizz paid no attention. He darted between the bushes and gates, peering over bins and rose twigs.

"Oi, tosser," Sarah really yelled this time.

"Where's Matt?" Frizz yelled back.

I was already beginning to feel a bit edgy, like frost was settling in my chest.

"Your guess," Sarah called.

"Where's Matt?" Frizz was stuck on repeat. "Where's Matt?"

Perhaps we all knew where Matt was, or perhaps we all took the hint of the direction given by one of us, because without saying anything we ran towards the river. Frizz kept calling for his brother as he ran. A snot bubble appeared out of his nose. He didn't bother to wipe it away.

I was the first to see Matt. Right on the bank where the river flowed over the grass. In the shade behind the trees.

The water was up to his ankles and in his hands he held that rug, the blue and green one. He swirled it up over his head and his body did this swaying thing like the reeds in the river, while his spare hand reached out to grab clean air which he clutched into his chest. His dance seemed to go on for hours and, as he gyrated, a plume of suspended droplets glistened above him in the air.

Then my mouth called, "Matt, hey Matt."

He jarred and twisted to see who was calling. When he spotted me, he smiled for a whole forever - Matt the Frost, Matt the Drip, Matt - before a gust of chill wind shattered hail down on him.

Mrs Gregory got there fast. Crunched through the ice that was already reforming to drag him back from the edge. And as she pulled the sodden rug from his hand and dashed it to the ground, Matt's face jerked the smile into sharp teeth and creases, and water cascaded out of his mouth down his chin.

Then Frizz did this thing. He grabbed his big brother round the waist, held his fingers interlocked until Mrs Gregory prised them apart and put an arm round each of them before leading them away.

I clamped my numb fingers under my armpits.

"Why didn't we dance with him?" I asked Sarah.

At least I hope I did.

Author Biography

Ruth Brandt enjoys exploring settings in her short stories, what they suggest to her about the inhabitants and the divisions they create – political, familial and the resulting intrapersonal conflicts.

Ruth has an MFA in Creative Writing from Kingston University where she won the MFA Creative Writing Prize 2016. She has been published by Aesthetica, Litro, Neon Magazine, Bridport Prize Anthology and many more, and was nominated for the Pushcart Prize and the Write Well Award in 2016, and Best Small Fictions 2019. She teaches creative writing, including at West Dean College, and was formerly Writer in Residence at the Surrey Wildlife Trust and the National Trust's Polesden Lacey.

Ruth's short story collection *No One Has Any Intention of Building a Wall* will be published by Fly on the Wall Press late 2021. She lives in Surrey with her hugely supportive husband and has two delightful sons.

Enjoy the rest of our 2021 Shorts Season:

Pigskin by David Hartley

Something strange is happening to the animals on the farm. A pig becomes bacon, chickens grow breadcrumbs, a cow turns to leather, a goat excretes cheese. As food becomes scarce and the looming 'pot-bellies' threaten to invade the safety of the sty, Pig knows he must get to the bottom of this strange phenomenon or face imminent death. Reminiscent of Animal Farm and darkly satirical, David Hartley interrogates the ethics of farming and the potential problems of genetic engineering, asking important questions about our relationship to the food – or animals – we eat.

"Pigskin is a knife-sharp, knowing fable about animal instincts and human ingenuity. David Hartley has a gift for creating stories that leave scars."

\- Aliya Whiteley, author of The Loosening Skin

PowerPoint Eulogy by Mark Wilson

Three corporate hours have been allotted to commemorate the life of enigma, Bill Motluck. Employee memories of his life are crudely recounted onto a dusty projector. No one has ever been quite sure of his purpose. No one is quite sure who wrote the PowerPoint...but it seems to be exposing them all, one by one.

"In his wildly imaginative chapbook, PowerPoint Eulogy, Chicago writer and visual artist Mark Wilson paints a picture of corporate culture—and humanity at large—that is both soul-crushingly bleak and hilariously demented. Divided into forty-four presentation "slides", the story centers on the memories a group of unnamed employees have of their recently deceased co-worker, Bill Motluck—a man so bland he enjoyed small talk about skim milk, and so desperate to fit in he once rented a newborn for Bring Your Kid to Work

Day. Should we give in to the impulse to laugh at poor Bill, or feel sympathy for his plight? As the stories and little revelations pile up, it becomes harder and harder to decide—and the tension this creates is what ultimately makes this one-of-a-kind collection so impossible to put down. I laughed, I winced, I loved it".

- Mark Rader, Author of 'The Wanting Life'.

Muscle and Mouth by Louise Finnigan

"A beautifully written and compelling story"

- Kerry Hudson, Award-Winning Author of 'Lowborn'

"Muscle and Mouth made me feel the fracture of my own northern identity deep in my gut. It made me ache for home. It reminded me that leaving a place means giving pieces of yourself away; your rawness, your language and a certain kind of love. Louise Finnigan is a writer to watch."

- Jessica Andews, Author of 'Saltwater' and Winner of 2020 Portico Prize

Jade is prepping an A-Level assignment, all her sights set on Durham University. She's told she has to 'prove herself' and keep her away from the unsavoury types she calls her best friends. Yet Jade is reluctant to shun her corner of Manchester, where she finds the land rich, 'dark with energy'.

How To Bring Him Back by Claire HM

'If I was going to cast a spell tonight, this night of a full arse moon as stark and crunchy as a ten-day crust of snow, I'd start by telling the earth to spin in the opposite direction.

By what power?

By the power of my pen.'

'How to Bring Him Back' is a journey into a darkly humorous

love triangle. It's 90s Birmingham and Cait is post-university, aimless and working in a dive bar. She's caught between Stadd, who's stable, funny, compatible as a friend, and her compulsive sexual attraction with Rik. Present day Cait picks up her pen, on her yearly writing retreat to Aberystwyth, and addresses an absent Stadd with the lessons she has learnt from her past.

Exploring the dynamics of desire and consent while reflecting upon the damage people can inflict on each other in relationships, Claire is an exciting and bold writer for the modern age.

The Guts of a Mackerel by Clare Reddaway

"Who's Bobby Sands?" she asked, as she laid the fish on the face of a smiling young man with long wavy hair. "And what's a hunger strike?"

On a family holiday to her dad's Irish homeland, Eve's concerns about impressing local boy Liam are confronted by the stark reality of political and personal divisions during the Troubles. Former friends have turned into enemies, and this country of childhood memory is suddenly a lot less welcoming.

About Fly on the Wall Press

A publisher with a conscience.
Publishing high quality anthologies on pressing issues,
chapbooks and poetry products, from exceptional poets
around the globe.
Founded in 2018 by founding editor, Isabelle Kenyon.

Other publications:

Please Hear What I'm Not Saying (February 2018. Anthology,
profits to Mind.)
Persona Non Grata (October 2018. Anthology, profits to
Shelter and Crisis Aid UK.)
Bad Mommy / Stay Mommy by Elisabeth Horan
(May 2019. Chapbook.)
The Woman With An Owl Tattoo by Anne Walsh Donnelly
(May 2019. Chapbook.)
the sea refuses no river by Bethany Rivers
(June 2019. Chapbook.)
White Light White Peak by Simon Corble
(July 2019. Artist's Book.)
Second Life by Karl Tearney
(July 2019. Full collection)
The Dogs of Humanity by Colin Dardis
(August 2019. Chapbook.)
Small Press Publishing: The Dos and Don'ts by Isabelle Kenyon
(January 2020. Non-Fiction.)
Alcoholic Betty by Elisabeth Horan
(February 2020. Full Collection.)
Awakening by Sam Love
(March 2020. Chapbook.)
Grenade Genie by Tom McColl
(April 2020. Full Collection.)

House of Weeds by Amy Kean and Jack Wallington
(May 2020. Full Collection.)
No Home In This World by Kevin Crowe
(June 2020. Short Stories.)
How To Make Curry Goat by Louise McStravick
(July 2020. Full Collection.)
The Goddess of Macau by Graeme Hall
(August 2020. Short Stories.)
The Prettyboys of Gangster Town by Martin Grey
(September 2020. Chapbook.)
The Sound of the Earth Singing to Herself by Ricky Ray
(October 2020. Chapbook.)
Mancunian Ways (Anthology of poetry and photography)
Inherent by Lucia Orellana Damacela
(November 2020. Chapbook.)
Medusa Retold by Sarah Wallis (December 2020. Chapbook.)
We Are All Somebody compiled by Samantha Richards (February
2021. Anthology. Profits to Street Child United.)
Pigskin by David Hartley (February 2021. Shorts.)
Aftereffects by Jiye Lee (March 2021. Chapbook.)
Someone Is Missing Me by Tina Tamsho-Thomas
(March 2021. Full Collection.)
PowerPoint Eulogy by Mark Wilson (April 2021. Shorts.)
Odd as F*ck by Anne Walsh Donnelly
(May 2021. Full collection.)
Muscle and Mouth by Louise Finnigan (June 2021. Shorts.)

Social Media:
@fly_press (Twitter)
@flyonthewall_poetry (Instagram)
@flyonthewallpress (Facebook)

Excerpt from 'No One Has Any Intention of Building A Wall' by Ruth Brandt
Short Story Collection
Released November 2021, Fly on the Wall Press

Petrification

Petrified night-trolls near Lake Ugly, 6th September 2014

The night-troll children were fishing down by the lake, dragging in net after net of salmon. So entranced were they by their bountiful haul that they forgot to keep an eye on the night sky. As the first glimmers of dawn infused the darkness, the mother troll rushed out of her cave to call her children to safety, only to discover them petrified. While she stared in shock, the morning light sloped on up the hill to strike her and she became petrified too.

So there they are, lumps of stone, one large boulder at the top gazing down at the smaller ones stuck forever on the shore of Lake Ugly.

We were told that story on the first day when we had yet to learn each others' names.

Volcanically heated pool at Landmannaglaugar, 6th September 2014

She stands in her swimming costume, water up to mid-thigh, her hand raised as though shielding her eyes from the sun. Except I don't remember the sun shining. I remember the wind later that night, strong enough to rattle the hut's corrugated iron roof as we lay in columns in our sleeping bags, surrounded by gentle breaths and ferocious snores. And I remember the snow the following morning that drove into our ears and nostrils as we trudged our way through the rhyolite mountains, the most dramatic scenery in Iceland, had we been able to see it through the blizzard.

Her face is dark beneath the shadow of her hand so that if this were the only photo I had of her, I would have nothing to remind me of her features. Perhaps she is waving. At me? At the group admiring the first person brave enough to get into the volcanic pool?

"Come on you lot," she is saying. "It's beautiful in here."

I hadn't expected the unevenness of the water's heat or the softness of the mud which moulded itself round my weary feet.

That first night she slept three people away from me. I noticed where she lay and as I said good night to everyone in general, I was really only saying good night to her.